Poppies for Amelia

PRAISE FOR *STORYSHARES*

"One of the brightest innovators and game-changers in the education industry."
– Forbes

"Your success in applying research-validated practices to promote literacy serves as a valuable model for other organizations seeking to create evidence-based literacy programs."
- Library of Congress

"We need powerful social and educational innovation, and Storyshares is breaking new ground. The organization addresses critical problems facing our students and teachers. I am excited about the strategies it brings to the collective work of making sure every student has an equal chance in life."
– Teach For America

"Around the world, this is one of the up-and-coming trailblazers changing the landscape of literacy and education."
- International Literacy Association

"It's the perfect idea. There's really nothing like this. I mean wow, this will be a wonderful experience for young people."   - Andrea Davis Pinkney, Executive Director, Scholastic

"Reading for meaning opens opportunities for a lifetime of learning. Providing emerging readers with engaging texts that are designed to offer both challenges and support for each individual will improve their lives for years to come. Storyshares is a wonderful start."
- David Rose, Co-founder of CAST & UDL

Poppies for Amelia

Julie Harris

STORYSHARES

Story Share, Inc.
New York. Boston. Philadelphia

Copyright © 2022 Julie Harris

All rights reserved.

Published in the United States by Story Share, Inc.

The characters and events in this book are fictitious. Any similarity to real persons, living or dead, is entirely coincidental.

Storyshares
Story Share, Inc.
24 N. Bryn Mawr Avenue #340
Bryn Mawr, PA 19010-3304
www.storyshares.org

Inspiring reading with a new kind of book.

Interest Level: High School
Grade Level Equivalent: 4.0

9781642614732

Book design by Storyshares

Printed in the United States of America

Storyshares Presents

1

The car came out of nowhere. I swerved to miss it, crashing through the neighbor's fence instead. I was only four houses away from home. Four houses away from having my father's truck back safe and sound. All I know is, if I hadn't been distracted by my thoughts at that very moment, I never would have met Saul Leiberman.

I knew Mr. Leiberman from walking by his house for the last two years, going to and from school. We had never even spoken. Most days, the old man was outside, tending to his yard and flower garden. The same flower's that were currently crushed beneath the tires of my father's beat up, old Chevy. Pieces of the white picket fence I'd busted through were scattered all around. I could tell this didn't make the old man happy as he came rushing out the front door, his face red and eyes all squinty.

Age spots dotted his bald head. His long, pointed nose, turned down into a white mustache and goatee that matched his bushy eyebrows. His dark brown eyes were brimming with anger. He was gesturing and speaking in a different language. As he got closer, he switched to English.

"My flowers! I work so hard! I know you! You're Nascha Hatahle, Shilah Hatahle's boy. You too young to drive. How old are you?"

"My name is Nash," I snapped back without thinking. (I didn't like being called by my full name.) I thought for a second of lying about my age and decided against it. "I'm fourteen."

"Just as I thought! Step out. Let me look at you."

I stepped out of the truck. I stood a good foot taller than the old man. His lean, slightly stooped frame was a contrast to my strong, broad shoulders. Mr. Leiberman seemed to be taking everything in. Everything from my black t-shirt to my jeans with the holes in the knees. He glanced down at my dirty, worn out sneakers. The look I usually get for being a Native American teenager was missing from the old man's face. After the initial once-over, he seemed to be searching deeper than outward appearances.

"What you plan to do now kid?"

I hung my head. My long black hair fell into my face, despite the bandanna around my forehead. "I can't afford to fix your fence, Mr. Leiberman. I'm sorry."

"Being sorry no good. You fix."

"I don't know how," I replied.

"A boy your age? Don't know how to repair a fence or plant flowers? Time to learn then. Come tomorrow morning, seven a.m. We start then."

"Seven a.m.!" Summer just started! This crazy old man thought I was going to get up that early? "No way!"

"Okay then. I call police. They take care of it. You have license?"

My shoulders slumped. I knew I was stuck. My father would kill me for sure if the police got involved. I hadn't exactly asked to borrow his truck.

I reluctantly agreed to come first thing in the morning. Sulking, I backed my father's rust bucket out of Mr. Leiberman's yard and headed home.

2

Mr. Leiberman had the garage door open and was already working away on something when I rode my skateboard up the next day. There was a small table with a saw on it. The old man was using it to cut lengths of wood.

"Two minutes late," he spoke as he shut the machine off, the saw slowly winding down.

I just shrugged. I didn't want to be here at all. Thankfully, my father hadn't noticed the small scratch and half-dollar sized dent in the truck. It had blended right in with all the other dents and scratches. I couldn't risk Mr. Leiberman turning me in though. Then I'd be in trouble with my father *and* the law.

"You know how to use one of these, right?" The old man was holding a push broom towards me. I took it and started sweeping up the wood shavings that covered the cement floor. The old man went to another table and began taking measurements of different pieces of wood.

We didn't speak much as the day wore on. It turned out, I was glad we had started so early. By eleven o'clock, the Arizona heat was already turning the small garage into an oven.

Mr. Leiberman had salvaged what wood he could from the broken fence. The old man also happened to have some spare wood from when he built the fence. He was using that for the rest of the repairs.

He wouldn't let me run the saw, so I was stuck sweeping and bringing him tools. He explained things as he went along. He said that we would have to paint the posts white to match the rest of the fence. We would do that before setting the posts. It would be easier and look neater.

At straight up noon, Mr. Leiberman sent me home. He said it was lunch time, and not much more could be done in the heat.

"Tomorrow, same time."

I sighed and agreed before taking off for home. Half the day gone. What a drag.

3

The next day was a little better.

Mr. Leiberman explained how he'd made the posts extra long, as they had to go two feet into the ground, to make them more stable.

"Won't hold up against a truck, though," he said with a wink. It was good he could joke about it.

All the posts and two by fours were ready to go from the day before, so we began making the pickets. A different tool was used to shape the tops. It was called a router. It was kind of neat watching Mr. Leiberman round the tops of the pickets. I hadn't given one thought to the hard work that went into making a fence. It had only taken a second to destroy it.

Again, at straight up noon, Mr. Leiberman called it a day. This time he invited me in for a sandwich and some lemonade. My stomach growled at the mere mention of food. My mouth was so dry it was hard to swallow.

The blast of cool air when we entered the house felt good on my skin. The sweat on the back of my shirt cooled instantly. Mr. Leiberman poured us both a glass of lemonade. He sent me into the dining room to wait while he made the sandwiches. Sipping the tangy, sweet drink, I found myself wandering a bit, curious as to how the old man lived. The dining room opened right up into the living area. The furnishings were sparse and worn, but the whole house was clean. So different from my own run down, messy heap.

A picture on an end table drew my attention. It was a photo of a young girl with short, dark hair. She must have been seven or eight years old. I thought maybe it was Mr. Leiberman's daughter, but then the picture was black and white and very old. Next to the picture frame was a small red flower. I touched it carefully, surprised to find that the cool, silky petals were real.

"Come and eat." Mr. Leiberman was in the doorway holding two plates with sandwiches. He had a stern look on his face. I followed him back into the dining room. I hoped the old man wasn't mad at me for snooping around. We ate in silence for a minute or two before I got up the nerve to ask about the picture. Mr. Leiberman's face closed up like a clam, making me wish I hadn't asked.

"That is not your business, son. Come back tomorrow. We'll work some more," and with that, Mr. Leiberman picked up his plate, rinsed it, and set it next to the sink.

"But tomorrow is Saturday!" Surely the old man didn't expect me to work on weekends too!

Mr. Leiberman seemed confused for a minute. "I'll see you first thing on Monday then. Don't be late."

I rinsed my plate and set it next to Mr. Leiberman's before heading out the door for home.

Poppies for Amelia

4

    I slept in the next day. I thought I'd be glad to be free from Mr. Leiberman's chores but found myself intrigued by the mysterious picture. I also found that I kind of missed the old man's company. I didn't have any friends. We lived on the wrong side of town, and I had a drunk for a dad. I didn't care to have other kids around, even if they wanted to be friends, which they didn't.

    I awoke and silently got dressed, being careful not to wake my father. I could hear his snores in the other room. He was obviously sleeping off last night's drunkeness. It was the only time he snored. I quietly slipped out the back door, grabbed my board, and took off towards the landfill.

I spent a lot of time at the landfill in the summer. It was mainly because I was less likely to run into other people there than in town. I found a lot of stuff that was still of good use there too, like my skateboard. Some kid had thrown it away just because it had a broken wheel. I'd fixed it and now had a faster way to get around.

I spent most of the day there, digging through the rubbish. I wasn't finding many treasures today. Finally giving up, I headed home.

I stopped short when I rolled up to the house. My father was sitting on the front porch with a bottle of cheap whiskey. He usually worked overtime at the Mill on Saturdays.

"Where you been all day boy?"

"Skateboarding downtown," I said.

"I've been downtown. Didn't see *you* anywhere. I'm tired of your lyin' boy!" He hurled the empty whiskey bottle at the sidewalk in front of my feet. Shards of glass flew everywhere.

"Always runnin' around. . . . You'll get in trouble one of these days . . . just another no good injun!"

I wanted to turn and ride away, but I knew I'd have to face him sooner or later. If I ran, I'd be in even more trouble when I got back. In a blink, my father was off the porch. He grabbed my board and threw it on the ground hard, causing it to crack. Grabbing the back of my neck in a death grip, he herded me up the front steps. He slammed the front door behind us with his foot, releasing my neck as he threw me towards the wall.

"I wanna know right now what kind of trouble you been gettin' into, boy!" He got right up in my face. The sour smell of whiskey washed over me in waves.

"I haven't been in any trouble." I braced myself for what I knew was coming next. The punch to my stomach didn't come as a surprise. I wasn't prepared for the fist to my face though. Blood spurted from my nose. My eye felt like it exploded in my face. I crumpled to the floor, protecting my body from further abuse.

"What a waste of space." He gave my side a swift kick and stormed out the door, probably in search of another bottle. I stayed where I was, crumpled on the floor until I was sure he was gone. A familiar feeling of hopelessness and lack of self-worth over-rode the physical pain.

5

Mr. Leiberman silently acknowledged my lack of skateboard and my black eye, but he didn't say a word. He just shook his head sadly and turned away, as if he knew exactly what had happened.

We spent most of the morning painting the posts, the two by fours, and the pickets. Mr. Leiberman used saw horses to hold the wood while we painted. We did this in the driveway so the paint fumes wouldn't get to us. As we finished each one, we set it carefully against the garage wall to dry. It was time-consuming, this fence building. At this rate, it was going to take all summer. I found I didn't mind as much as before.

After painting the last picket, we ventured out to the fence line. Mr. Leiberman had already cleaned up the damage. The fence was ready for rebuilding. We took measurements and re-dug the holes where the new posts would go.

Again, Mr. Leiberman invited me in for lunch. He made small talk while we ate. He asked me how I did in school and what I wanted to do when I grew up. No one had shown any interest in my life for a while now. It was strange. Then he asked about my mother. I was surprised to find myself answering him.

"My mother died two years ago, from cancer. We had no money for the medical care she needed. The medicine man on the reservation did all that he could. It was not enough. After she died, my father decided to move here."

It was the most I'd ever said on the subject. It had also been when my father's drinking had gotten out of control, but that was more than I wanted to share. Mr. Leiberman seemed to understand that I didn't want to talk about it anymore. He just nodded sadly and changed the subject.

"You don't have many friends, do you?" he asked bluntly.

I shook my head. "People judge me harshly because I'm different."

"What, you mean sullen and angry, with no self-esteem?"

I shot a dirty look his way.

"I'm just teasing you. You see, I too, know about loss. I also know about being treated unfairly just for being who you are. You asked about the picture the last time you were here. The girl in the picture was my twin sister."

I stayed silent, hoping he would go on.

6

"Her name was Amelia." Mr. Leiberman paused for a minute as if deciding whether to continue. Then he did something unexpected. He pushed his sleeve up, revealing faint, tattooed numbers. I thought to myself, *why is he showing me an old tattoo?* I didn't have any myself, so he couldn't lecture me on getting ink. Why would he get a tattoo of a bunch of numbers anyway? His next words were my answer.

"German soldiers did this to me. The day they did this I became just a number, instead of a real person. Over six million people died, simply because they were

Jewish. My mother, father, and sister Amelia were part of that number."

I had heard of the Holocaust, but I had never met a single person who had been a part of it. All I knew was that a man named Adolf Hitler had been the reason a lot of people died. I was blown away that Mr. Leiberman had actually been there. I thought of it as a part of history. After all, this was 2010. It seemed like something that had happened in another lifetime.

Mr. Leiberman was watching me closely before continuing. "My father and I were separated from my mother and sister and taken to different work camps. I never saw them again. My father and I went to a camp called Dachau. They fed us barely enough to stay alive, and worked us past exhaustion. My father died one year later from pneumonia. I learned later that both my mother and sister had died as well. Amelia was shot by German soldiers for not working fast enough . . . she had collapsed with exhaustion. When my mother went to her, they shot her too."

I felt a lump in my throat. What it must have been like to lose your whole family that way! I thought of the way the other kids treated me. How minor in comparison it was to what Mr. Leiberman had been through. I pictured the hate in others' eyes when they scorned me just for being different. I now had a mental picture of just how far that hate could go when out of control.

"Anyway, the poppy next to the frame is in remembrance of my Amelia and the many others who died. I put a fresh one next to her picture every day."

A memory flashed through my head. The flower's that had been crushed under the wheels of my father's truck—they looked just like the poppy next to Amelia's picture!

I hung my head in shame. I'd had never felt so bad about anything in my life. Mr. Leiberman seemed to understand.

"Don't worry child. We replant and grow. Life goes on for those of us here. Tomorrow, you help with planting?"

Incapable of speech, I just nodded sadly.

"If you're done with your sandwich, you may go." I hadn't even realized I'd only eaten half of my sandwich. Mr. Leiberman lifted my chin gently with one finger. "It's okay child. Do not feel bad for things that can't be changed. Come tomorrow, and help an old man replant." I sensed a double meaning to his words.

"I'll see you tomorrow at seven, Mr. Leiberman."

"Call me Saul."

I looked at Mr. Leiberman with surprise. I'd had never even known the man's first name. Mr. Leiberman/Saul smiled gently as I walked out the door.

7

As soon as I got to Saul's house the next morning, he had me run home and get my skateboard. I told him it was broken, but he said to get it anyway. When I returned, he showed me how to make another one with a piece of scrap. When he was done, it looked kinda plain, so he let me paint it. I put a lightning bolt down the middle. I was relieved that he didn't ask how it got broken.

We went to work digging up the ruined poppies and got the soil ready for planting. Saul said we needed to wait for the paint on the fence to dry anyway, so this was a good time to start on the garden. It was still weird, calling Mr. Leiberman by his first name. We used our hands to dig small holes for planting, then sprinkled the tiny seeds along the surface of the fresh earth. Then we covered the tops lightly with soil.

Saul said they were supposed to be planted in late fall, and it was really too early to plant. He said we'd start another one later, but he'd always been curious if they'd grow any other time. After we were done, he showed me how to use a watering can to water gently, so as not to flush the seeds away.

We decided to have lunch while the paint on my board dried. Saul talked some more about the war and the camp he and his father had been in.

"Amelia and I were only ten years old. We were lucky the soldiers didn't realize we were twins."

He explained how their mother had instinctively held back when they called out 'Zwillinge', the German word for twins. Saul spoke of injections and horrific experiments that he learned later were done on over three thousand twins. Out of that number, only two hundred had survived the experiments.

"The soldiers had no compassion. If you were sick or too weak to work, you were shot without a second thought. Small children and infants were taken away from their families as soon as we got off the train. I could not understand why. Turns out they were taken to be killed. They were of no use to the Germans. They couldn't work and needed care and supervision."

Saul talked for an hour before we decided the paint would be dry enough to attach the wheels to the new board. After measuring, and screwing the old wheels on the new board he said to give it a try.

I rode up and down the sidewalk doing spins and turns, amazed at how well it rode. I thanked Saul and waved as I took off for home.

Poppies for Amelia

8

The next day, I didn't go right home as usual. I had a lot on my mind. Two years ago, today, was the day my mother had died. Instead of going home, I walked to the cemetery at the edge of town. My mother had been buried on the reservation in New Mexico, but my father had a marker put here in Arizona so we would have a place to visit.

As I rode into the cemetery, I immediately noticed someone in front of her marker. That was strange. Who would be there besides father and me? Father would be at the mill still, and he usually went to the bar after work.

As I approached, my stomach did a flip as I realized that it was, in fact, my father. He was sitting cross-legged on the ground in front of my mother's grave. I turned to go, not wanting to fight with him today.

"Nascha," my father called out to me. "Come." He waved me over to him. I had no choice now. I'd been spotted. I made my way past the other graves to the spot on the hill under the tree, where my mother's marker was.

My father seemed to have aged overnight. His black hair was clean and brushed, blowing gently in the breeze. The lines in his face seemed deeper. I was thrown off balance to see that his eyes were red as if he'd been crying. I'd only ever seen my father cry one time. To my even greater surprise, he seemed completely sober. I stood next to him, not knowing how to act. He patted the ground, and I kneeled beside him.

"Your mother loved you very much, you know," he paused for composure. "Her love was bigger than both of us." I didn't know how to respond. My father could often be unpredictable when he was drinking, and he hadn't been sober in so long, I didn't know how to act with him.

"It was your mother who gave you the name Nascha." My father looked straight ahead, still gazing at her marker. "Did she ever tell you what it means?"

"No," I answered softly, my head down.

"It is a Navajo name meaning owl. It was the first thing she saw as you came into the world." My father turned and looked into my eyes. There was a soft expression on his face. "She said it was perfect for you, as an owl is wise and that you, too, would be wise."

"I never knew that."

"There is so much that you don't know. I'm sure you know how much your mother loved you, but what you may not know, son, is how much you are loved by me." A tear rolled down his cheek. I jumped a little when he touched the side of my face, but for once, his touch was gentle. He ran his thumb lightly over my blackened eye and bruised cheek. "I don't always know how to show it." His regret was plain to see.

I couldn't stop the tears that flowed silently down my face. What he said next filled me with a hope that had been long gone from me.

"Nascha, I want to stop the drinking and be a real father to you again. It is what your mother would want, and it is what I want."

"I want that too." My words were almost a whisper. I wasn't sure he heard me, until he turned and wrapped me in an embrace. I couldn't remember the last time my father had hugged me. We stayed like that for what seemed like forever before he let go. He motioned that we get up off the ground. I had to help him up. He said he'd been sitting there for awhile, and his bones weren't as young as they used to be. We walked out of the cemetery together, my heart filled with hope for the first time in a really long time.

9

The rest of the summer flew by. My father stayed true to his word and didn't drink. Things weren't perfect between us. It took awhile to adjust to our new roles. He came straight home after work. We took turns making something to eat for supper. Sometimes it was hard for me, having someone to answer to in the evenings. Before, I had been free to do pretty much what I wanted to all day. There hadn't been anyone who cared where I was or what I was doing.

One evening, my father asked what I did during the day, while he was at work. He seemed sincere, so I told him about working for Saul Leiberman. When I told him about crashing the truck, I thought he'd be angry.

He hung his head and simply said, "You are repaying your debt. That is what matters."

Saul and I finished building the fence and watered the garden every day. I still felt bad about ruining his flowers, but there were still enough good ones to put by Amelia's picture every day until the new ones grew. The ones we had planted were showing small sprouts. They barely showed above the soil. You had to look close.

I learned a lot from Saul that summer. He taught me the value of hard work and to be respectful of others. We had both lost people we love and both had been very lonely.

Fall moved in quicker than I would have liked. Saul and I started another small garden of poppies, this one in the backyard. Away from the road. He said it was just a precaution. I was worried that when I started back to school, Saul wouldn't need me anymore.

The day before school started, we stood under the shade tree next to the garage, admiring the new fence.

We watched the yellow and orange leaves fall, scattering on the ground around us.

"Nash . . . You come after school, tomorrow? We'll rake leaves?"

The smile stretched all the way across my face. "Call me Nascha. As soon as the last bell rings, I'll be here."

About The Author

Julie Harris is a wife and a mother of one. She's had three poems published and recently received her diploma in creative writing. She is working towards a goal of writing novels for a living. This Storyshares contest appealed to her because of the possibility of helping others learn to read and enjoy the magical world of written stories.

Poppies for Amelia

About The Publisher

Story Shares is a nonprofit focused on supporting the millions of teens and adults who struggle with reading by creating a new shelf in the library specifically for them. The ever-growing collection features content that is compelling and culturally relevant for teens and adults, yet still readable at a range of lower reading levels.

Story Shares generates content by engaging deeply with writers, bringing together a community to create this new kind of book. With more intriguing and approachable stories to choose from, the teens and adults who have fallen behind are improving their skills and beginning to discover the joy of reading. For more information, visit storyshares.org.

Easy to Read. Hard to Put Down.

Made in the USA
Middletown, DE
21 January 2023

22080196R10028